THE AWKWARD DINOSAURS

WRITTEN & ILLUSTRATED by
KELLEN ROGGENBUCK

KR PUBLISHING

ISBN: 978-0-578-79910-0

DINOSAURS

HAVE YOU HEARD OF THE DINOSAURS?
STEGOSAURUS OR TYRANNOSAURUS REX?
WELL, THERE ARE A FEW OTHER DINOSAURS
OUT THERE THAT DON'T GET MUCH ATTENTION.
THEY ARE NICE AND HAVE GOOD PERSONALITIES
AND ARE USUALLY ON TIME TO A PARTY.

THIS BOOK IS ALL ABOUT THE
AWKWARD DINOSAURS.

DISTRACTICUS TINIUS

THESE TINY DINOSAURS ARE USUALLY NOT PAYING ATTENTION bECAUSE OF A NEARbY SHINY ROCK OR ANOTHER DINOSAUR burPING.

MUSTACHASAURUS

THIS AWKWARD DINOSAUR HAS A MYSTERIOUSLY THICK MUSTACHE AND EYE bROWS. HE CARRIES A LARGE COMb TO KEEP IT CLEAR OF FOOD AND SMALLER ANIMALS.

HULATALLULA REX

THE MOST DIFFICULT PART OF THIS DINOSAUR'S DAY IS FINDING GRASS SKIRTS IN HER SIZE, BUT SHE HAS EXCELLENT RHYTHM AND GRACE.

SELFIESTICKADON

MUCH IS KNOWN ABOUT THIS AWKWARD DINO BECAUSE OF ALL THE PICTURES HE TOOK OF HIMSELF. HE'S KNOWN TO BE ALWAYS ASKING IF ANYONE HAS A PHONE CHARGER HANDY.

GLOWbISAURUS

THIS INTERESTING DINOSAUR'S SKELETON GLOWS THROUGH HIS SKIN. IT MEANS HE'S GREAT TO HAVE NEAR IF YOU ARE AFRAID OF THE DARK AND HE'S TERRIBLE AT HIDE-AND-GO-SEEK.

HEADADON AND REACHYDACTYL

HEADADON HAS A LARGE HEAD THAT IT CAN HARDLY HOLD UP, bUT HIS FRIEND REACHYDACTYL HELPS HIM OUT. THEY ALSO LIKE PLAYING CHECKERS.

OPTOMISAURUS

THIS AWKWARD DINOSAUR CAN'T SEE WITHOUT HIS THICK GLASSES WHICH ARE HARD TO KEEP ON SINCE HE DOESN'T HAVE ANY EARS.

TALLISAURUS

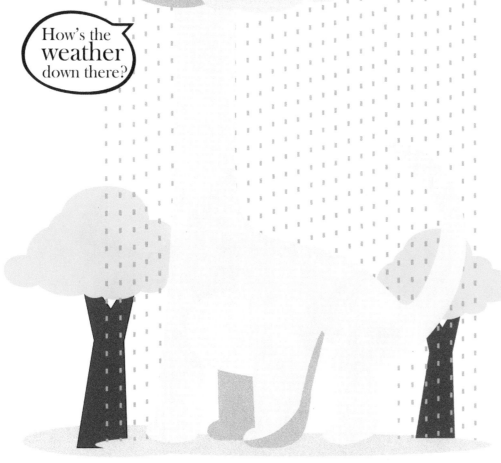

TALLISAURUS ALWAYS HAS HER HEAD IN THE CLOUDS,
WHICH IS GOOD BECAUSE SHE LOVES WEATHER!

PLAIDIPUS REX

PLAIDIPUS REX IS A FRIENDLY DINOSAUR WHO KEEPS WARM IN THE WINTER MONTHS, bUT YOU WON'T FIND HER HANGING OUT WITH THE POLKADOTADON, THEY TEND TO CLASH.

SNEEZIESNOTUS

I think it's just allergies

YOU CAN HEAR THE TRUMPETING SNEEZES ACROSS THE JUNGLE FROM THIS AWKWARD DINOSAUR. SHE WILL bE HAPPY TO LEND YOU A TISSUE iF YOU NEED iT!

SHYLADON

This is fine. I'm fine.

THIS SHY DINOSAUR ISN'T A FAN OF LARGE CROWDS. IN FACT, SHE USUALLY DOESN'T LEAVE HER SHELL AND LIVES IN HER OWN COZY EGG FORT.

POKIEHORNIDON

I'm not much of a hugger.

DON'T GET TOO CLOSE TO THIS AWKWARD DINO! HE'S GOT HORNS ALL OVER HIS BODY THAT HE USES TO HELP ITCH THE BELLIES OF BIGGER DINOSAURS.

SHOUTASAURUS

THIS DINOSAUR IS KNOWN FOR HIS big
PERSONALITY AND EVEN bigger VOICE!
HE ISN'T VERY good AT WHISPERING but
HE'S quick TO SAY SOMETHING NICE.

LOWLADACTYL

THIS AWKWARD DINOSAUR HAS TINY WINGS AND CAN ONLY FLY A FEW FEET ABOVE THE GROUND. SHE ALSO HAS A LOVELY SINGING VOICE.

PIERRASAURUS

PIERRASAURUS IS NEVER CAUGHT WITHOUT HIS SIGNATURE BERET, HE HAS A COLLECTION OF A DOZEN. HE ALSO LOVES TO WEAR BEANIES AND SOMBREROS ON RAINY DAYS.

SNORKELADON

THE LARGEST AWKWARD WATER DINOSAUR,
SHE IS A GRACEFUL SWIMMER. bUT, bECAUSE
OF HER SNORKEL, IT'S HARD TO UNDERSTAND
WHAT SHE'S SAYING.

BLANKASAUR

trust me, I'm here.

BLANKASAUR IS A RARE FIND IN THE WILD BECAUSE HE IS SO LIGHT IN COLOR AND ENJOYS WINTER SPORTS. THIS IS PROBABLY A PICTURE OF HIM.

WHETHER OR NOT THEY ARE IN THE HISTORY BOOKS, THESE AWKWARD DINOSAURS WERE A HAPPY BUNCH! THEY KNEW WHO THEY WERE AND WERE HAPPY BEING THEMSELVES.

THAT'S WHY THE AWKWARD DINOSAURS
WERE THE COOLEST DINOS AROUND!.

SO IF YOU ARE DISTRACTED bY bURPING DINOS
OR IF YOU TRY TO TALK TO YOUR FRIENDS WITH
A SNORKEL IN YOUR MOUTH,

YOU CAN bE HAPPY TO kNOW THAT YOU ARE JUST LİkE ONE OF THE MANY AWkWARD DİNOSAURS.

..AND THAT'S PRETTY COOL.

THE END.

BE SURE TO CHECK OUT OTHER BOOKS BY AUTHOR KELLEN ROGGENBUCK:

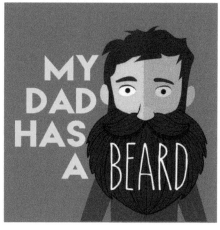

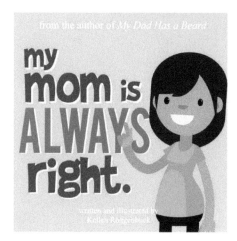

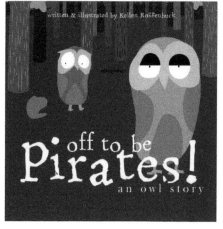

EACH BOOK IS WRITTEN TO BE FUN AND ENGAGING FOR READERS ADULT AND CHILDREN ALIKE, AND ARE AVAILABLE ON AMAZON!

CPSIA information can be obtained
at www.ICGtesting.com
Printed in the USA
LVHW072344101120
671363LV00022B/1396

9 780578 799100